Disney
FROZEN II
Read-Along
STORYBOOK AND CD

Queen Elsa and Princess Anna, along with their friends, journey far beyond Arendelle to an enchanted forest. To find out what happens, read along with me in your book. You will know it's time to turn the page when you hear this sound. . . . Let's begin now.

Published by Disney Press, an imprint of Disney Book Group. No part of this book may be reproduced or transmitted in any form or by any means, electronic or mechanical, including photocopying, recording, or by any information storage and retrieval system, without written permission from the publisher. For information address Disney Press, 1200 Grand Central Avenue, Glendale, California 91201.

Printed in the United States of America

First Paperback Edition, October 2019   10 9 8 7 6 5 4 3 2 1

Library of Congress Control Number: 2019939776

FAC-038091-19231

ISBN 978-1-368-04280-2

For more Disney Press fun, visit www.disneybooks.com

DISNEY PRESS
Los Angeles • New York

SUSTAINABLE FORESTRY INITIATIVE

Certified Sourcing
www.sfiprogram.org
SFI-00993

Logo Applies to Text Stock Only

When Queen Elsa and Princess Anna were children, their parents often told them stories about the past. One night King Agnarr told them about the Northuldra, people from an enchanted forest.

The Northuldra had lived in harmony with the people of Arendelle, but then everything changed, and the two sides went to war. Angered spirits trapped both groups in the forest, but King Agnarr managed to escape.

After the story, Queen Iduna soothed the girls with a lullaby. "When I was little, my mother would sing a song about a special river called Ahtohallan that was said to hold all the answers about the past, about what we are a part of. . . ."

Many years had passed since those days, and though their parents were gone, the girls had found family in their best friends, Kristoff, Sven, and Olaf. They spent countless evenings together hanging out, having dinner, and playing games.

One night, during charades, Anna struggled to guess what Elsa was acting out. "Teeth? Ooh, pillow fort?" She could tell something was bothering her sister. "Disturbed. Oh, come on, you definitely look disturbed. Are you okay?" Elsa forced a smile before going upstairs. "Definitely. Just tired."

Moments later Anna went to check on Elsa. "You're wearing Mother's scarf. You do that when something's wrong."

Though Elsa refused to admit it, something *was* wrong. Someone—or something—was calling to her. It seemed as though no one else could hear it, but it tugged at her, as if trying to draw her out of the kingdom. Though she tried with all her might, she couldn't silence it.

Later that night, Elsa found herself answering the mysterious voice, singing along with it, and trying to follow it. She couldn't help wondering . . . did the voice belong to someone magical, like her?

As she began using her powers, she could feel them changing. They grew stronger and stronger until she sent out an enormous blast that caused a shock wave across the kingdom. Fire vanished from the torches; the fountains and waterfalls dried up; the wind even died.

Villagers stumbled over the rippling cobblestones, and everyone headed for stable ground. "Head for the cliffs!"

Once everybody was safe above Arendelle, Elsa told Anna about the voice she'd been hearing.

Just then, the ground rumbled. "I know that rumble."

Boulders rolled in and popped open, revealing trolls. Grand Pabbie quickly approached the girls. He explained that Elsa had woken the spirits of the Northuldra Forest.

Pabbie told Elsa to follow the voice north. Then he quietly told
Anna that she should go along to protect her sister.

"I won't leave her side."

Olaf, Sven, and Kristoff all agreed to join Elsa, too.

"We'll fix it together."

"Together."

"Together."

When they found the forest entrance, Olaf bounced against a
wall of mist that surrounded it. "Um, I sense no way in, but this is
fun nonetheless."

Elsa and Anna joined hands, and the mist seemed to part before them. They led the group through. But when they pushed on the mist from inside the forest, it pushed back. "Huh. It let us in, but it clearly does not want to let us out."

It wasn't long before the Wind Spirit, Gale, appeared. It picked them all up and whipped them around and around.

Anna closed her eyes. "I think I'm gonna be sick!"

Elsa used her powers to force everyone out of the wind vortex, but she was stuck inside. She sent out one final blast of magic to free herself, and beautiful ice sculptures appeared. Each one captured a different moment in time. Elsa had never created anything like them before!

Olaf shared his theory about how ice could reveal the past. "Water has memory."

It wasn't long before reindeer surrounded them and people dropped from the trees. Then soldiers appeared. They were the trapped Northuldra and Arendellians from Anna and Elsa's old bedtime story!

Both sides tried to claim the group as their prisoners. "Run!"

But Elsa used her powers, shocking everyone and sending them to the ground.

Anna recognized one of the soldiers. "Lieutenant Mattias! Third floor, second portrait on the left. You were our father's official guard."

Mattias couldn't believe it. "Your father was—"

"King Agnarr of Arendelle."

Mattias was overjoyed to hear that the king had made it out of the forest.

Then the Northuldra noticed that the sisters' scarf was Northuldran.

They realized that whoever had saved the king from the forest must have been a Northuldra! The idea that the two opposing sides had come together that day startled both the Arendellians and the Northuldra. They believed Elsa's magic was the key to their freedom.

They crowded around her with great anticipation, smothering her and overwhelming her with their expectations, until a bright flash of fire appeared.

The Fire Spirit dashed around the trees, setting them ablaze. Elsa used her magic to chase it down and discovered the spirit was a small salamander. It snuggled into her cold hand. "Ooh! Ow. Ow."

The voice called, and Elsa and the salamander both turned toward it. "You hear it, too?" The salamander looked into the distance. Elsa recalled Pabbie's advice. "Okay, keep going north."

Anna ran to Elsa when the mayhem had calmed, and the sisters embraced.

"Are you okay?"

"I'm fine. I—I just . . . actually, I'm starving."

As everyone enjoyed stew and glogg, Mattias talked with Anna. She confessed to him that she was worried about Elsa, and told him of her greatest fear: "If I lost her, I think I'd lose myself."

Mattias told her that loss actually just helped people understand what they were made of.

Meanwhile, one of the Northuldra was explaining the symbols on the scarf to Elsa. "All this time, the four spirits, right there." The Northuldran woman pointed out a fifth spirit, which was called the bridge, and explained that it disappeared when people stopped listening.

"You mean like a voice?" Elsa was now certain that she had to follow the call to set everyone free.

Kristoff and Sven had gone with one of the Northuldra to help with their reindeer, and Elsa refused to wait. Anna was sad to leave Kristoff, but unable to let Elsa go alone, she and Olaf joined Elsa, and the three continued north. When they reached the top of a hill, they gasped at the sight below. "Mother and Father's ship."

They realized this must mean that their parents had been in search of Ahtohallan when they disappeared. "This is my fault. They were going there looking for answers about me." Elsa vowed to find the mysterious river, even if it meant crossing the dangerous Dark Sea.

Despite Anna's protesting, Elsa
had to go alone. She waved her
hands, creating a boat, and sent
Anna and Olaf sliding down a path
of ice.

"Elsa, what are you doing? No,
no!" They couldn't stop, and soon
they found themselves gliding down
a river.

Anna noticed Earth Giants
sleeping on the shore.

"They're huge."

"Hang on, Olaf." Using a
branch, she directed their boat away
from the Earth Giants and over a
waterfall.

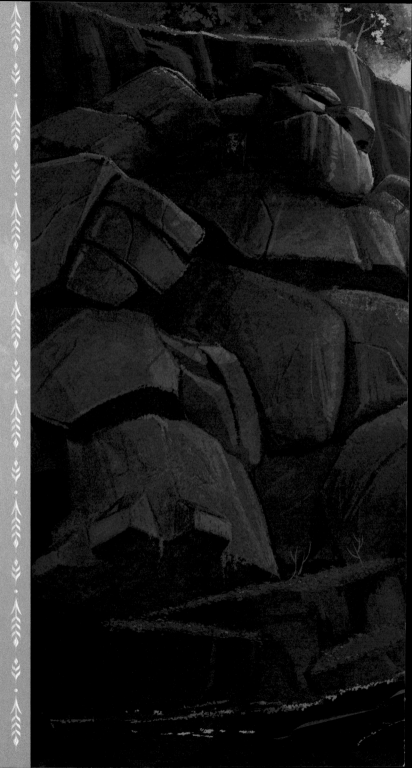

When Elsa reached the Dark Sea, she stood on the shore. Ferocious waves rose and crashed before her. She sprinted out onto the water, creating frozen snowflakes at her feet. But the strength of the waves quickly knocked her down. Then she tried freezing the water, but bigger waves knocked her back into the sea. Elsa clawed her way to the surface and climbed up on a giant rock. She took a breath and dove in.

The Water Nokk, an enormous horse, emerged and began tossing her around.
Elsa created an ice bridle and swung onto its back. At first it bucked, trying
to throw her off, but before long the two were rhythmically riding through the
mountainous waves to the far shore.

The waterfall had carried Anna and Olaf into a cavern. As they searched for a way out, a small flurry of snowflakes rushed in. It fluttered around before vanishing. Anna's heart filled with joy. "She made it across the sea."

Then a strong gust of wind whipped in, carrying more of Elsa's magic, and an ice sculpture formed before them, revealing a memory of the past.

Anna gasped. "I know why the spirits evacuated Arendelle. Olaf, I know how to free the forest." Armed with renewed strength and wisdom, Anna was ready to set things right.

Elsa trudged through terrible winds and thick snow. When she finally reached Ahtohallan, the mysterious voice quieted. Suddenly, just as the words of her mother's lullaby had promised, everything became crystal clear. Elsa knew she had followed the right path and was where she was meant to be.

The journey had changed both her and her sister. And together, they could restore peace and mend a broken land.